MW01103966

Kichi in Jungle Jeopardy

Kichi in Jungle Jeopardy

By Lila Guzmán
Illustrations by Regan Johnson

Blooming Tree Press
Austin, Texas

Kichi in Jungle Jeopardy

Blooming Tree Press
PO Box 140934
Austin, TX 78714-0934
www.bloomingtreepress.com

Cover art and interior illustrations by Regan Johnson
Cover design by Kelly Bell
Editing and book design by Madeline Smoot
Copyediting by Megan Dietsche

Library of Congress Cataloging-in-Publication Data

Guzmán, Lila, 1952-
Kichi in jungle jeopardy / by Lila Guzman ; illustrated by Regan Johnson.
p. cm.
Summary: After learning of a plot by the jungle animals to start a war between the Mayan humans, a rare blue Chihuahua dog named Kichi tries to
foil the scheme by finding the only person he knows who can speak Dog.
ISBN 0-9769417-1-6 (hardcover) -- ISBN 0-9769417-2-4 (pbk.)
[1. Chihuahua (Dog breed)--Fiction. 2. Jungle animals--Fiction. 3. Human-
animal relationships--Fiction. 4. Dogs--Fiction. 5. Mayas--Fiction. 6. Indians
of Central America--Fiction.] I. Johnson, Regan, 1975- ill. II. Title.

PZ7.G9885Kic 2006
[Fic]--dc22
2006001691

Printed in the United States of America
Text set in Warnock Pro

This book is dedicated to dogs everywhere.

Special thanks to:
Chip, Sammy, Chance and Lucy

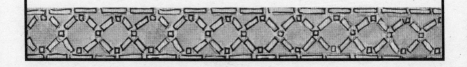

Chapter One

One steamy summer morning, the emperor's Fortune-Teller carried me outside for fresh air and placed me on a plump pillow. He tickled me under the chin and asked in a baby voice: "Would Sugar like some armadillo meat?"

"I'd prefer some pleasant conversation," I said. "And my name's not Sugar. It's Kichi."

His face remained blank as he fed me a piece of roasted armadillo.

I chewed on it and sighed. As usual, he hadn't understood a word I said. I might as well have been speaking Jaguar. No matter how hard I tried, I couldn't teach him my language. It wasn't his fault. Humans are rather dull-witted and simply cannot speak Dog.

Or so I thought until — but, wait. I'm getting ahead of myself.

So there I was, chewing armadillo meat in front of the Temple of the Two-Headed Snake, the largest building in Chilaam. When my stomach was full, I rested my head on crossed paws and scanned the main plaza and the emerald lawn that stretched from pyramid to pyramid.

In the nearby jungle, monkeys shrieked, making me glad that they were there and I was here. I had never been out of the capital and I planned to keep it that way.

I was born in a cotton-lined basket two years ago, the only bluish gray puppy in the litter. The birth of a rare blue chihuahua was hailed as a sign of good luck. Priests immediately designated me a sacred temple dog to be pampered and spoiled and fed the best food.

Still, I wondered. Was I to be a pet all my life? Or could I be something more?

No city in the Mayan Empire is quite like Chilaam. Morning, noon and night, it swarms with people. Today, noblemen played ball in the court to my left. To my right, workers chiseled designs on the steps of the new pyramid.

Not a hint of a breeze stirred in the city, so my keeper sat beside me, fanning me with a palm leaf.

I heard the tramp of approaching feet.

I smelled the soldiers even before they came into view. Every human has a special odor. Potters smell like mud. Cooks smell like cornmeal cakes. Soldiers smell like blood.

The emperor's guard, coming back from a raid, strode into the plaza. Behind them came captives with hands tied behind their backs.

I felt sorry for them, for I knew their fate. People of little importance would become slaves. The rest would be sacrificed to the gods. If one of them happened to be a king or prince, he would be the first to die.

One captive in particular caught my eye. A boy about twelve summers old stumbled along in the center of the caravan. He wore only one sandal. His eyes darted left and right, taking in the grandeur of Chilaam. He seemed impressed with our pyramids, the tallest in the empire.

But the thing that struck me as odd was his forehead. Unlike the other captives, his hadn't been shaped when he was a baby to slope backwards. Humans considered a slanting forehead a sign of great beauty.

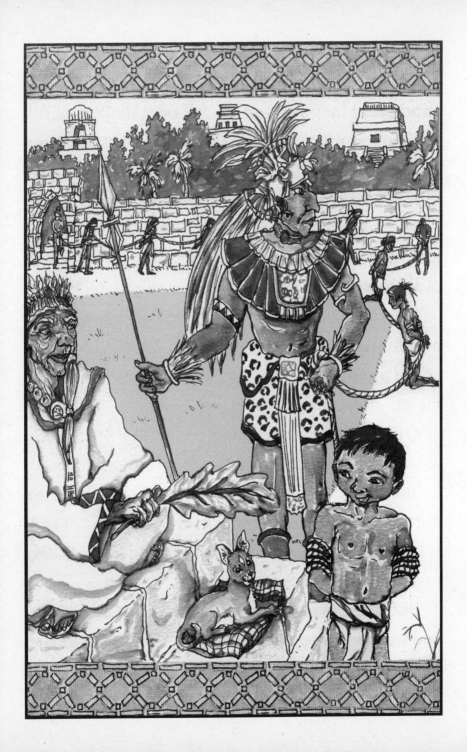

He stopped and stared straight at me. Offering me a half smile, he grunted hello. Not just any "hello," mind you. He spoke Dog.

This was most shocking. Before I could respond, Ah Tok, captain of the emperor's guard and Fortune-Teller's brother, shoved the boy forward.

The captives bristled and circled him protectively. It reminded me of a mother bird spreading her wings over the nest to protect her babies.

I just had to talk to that boy. I jumped down from my pillow.

Fortune-Teller was too fast for me. He scooped me up and held me tight to his chest. "Be careful, Sugar," he cooed. "You could break a bone and I'd be in sooooooo much trouble."

That was true. Anyone who hurt me or let me get hurt would be severely punished.

"I want that boy!" I whined as I quivered with excitement.

Fortune-Teller thought I was shivering with cold and wrapped me in a blanket.

"I didn't ask for my blanket," I barked. "I want that boy!"

The god-who-hears-dog-prayers must have been listening. The other captives were led off, but Ah Tok brought him over.

"Dearest brother!" Ah Tok exclaimed as he grasped Fortune-Teller by the upper arms. "You are looking well."

"As are you. May the gods be praised for your safe return."

Ah Tok untied the boy. "They smiled on me this time, brother! I captured five slaves. I can sell them and finally have enough cocoa beans to get out of debt."

"What do you plan to do with him?" Fortune-Teller nodded toward the boy.

"Uxmal? I haven't quite decided."

Fortune-Teller cradled me in his arms. That put me at eye level with the boy.

"I can't believe you speak Dog," I whined.

"I can," the boy whined back.

It was too good to be true. To test him, I said, "I adore being scratched between my ears and eyes."

The boy reached toward me.

6

Ah Tok's arm shot out and grabbed him by the scruff of the neck. "Never touch the sacred temple dog."

I squirmed, whined, and wagged my tail.

Fortune-Teller had trouble holding onto me. "He seems to like you," he said to Uxmal. "Usually, I don't let anyone touch him, but you may pet him just this once."

Ah Tok released Uxmal. "Don't abuse my brother's generosity."

The boy gently rubbed that special place between my ears and eyes.

A big smile stretched across my face...and his.

"I like to be tickled under my chin," I said.

"Is this the right spot?"

"You *can* understand me! At last! Someone who speaks Dog. How did you learn my language?"

The boy grinned and shrugged. "It just came naturally."

The conversation ended between the two brothers. They hugged and said good-bye.

"Come, slave!" Ah Tok said sharply.

Anger flashed from the boy's eyes. "My name is Uxmal."

Ah Tok slapped him.

The blow hit Uxmal so hard he reeled backwards and fell. His hand flew to his stinging cheek. He looked shocked, as if he had never been struck before.

It hurt to see my friend mistreated. I struggled out of Fortune-Teller's arms and dashed over to Uxmal. I licked his face to comfort him.

Fists on his hips, Ah Tok stood over the boy and glared down at him. "A slave does not speak until spoken to. You belong to me now and you will never use that tone of voice with me again." Ah Tok turned and dragged the boy away.

I was sad to see Uxmal leave. At last I had found a human who understood me! Unfortunately, he was Ah Tok's slave. I had to do something to change that.

Chapter Two

The next morning, Fortune-Teller decided to visit his brother who lived on the far side of the city. He carried me in his arms and wove in and out of teeming crowds. Along the way we passed beekeepers tending their hives and farmers driving their turkeys and ducks toward holding pens behind the emperor's palace.

Dead Time was near. Humans never took a trip, planted a crop, or married during these five unlucky days at the end of the year. To prepare for it, they held elaborate feasts and sacrificed to the gods.

Uxmal was planting seeds in Ah Tok's herb garden when we arrived.

"Where's my brother?" Fortune-Teller asked.

"Your esteemed brother was called to the palace," Uxmal replied.

"I'll wait." Fortune-Teller lowered himself carefully to the stone steps and sat in the shade of an avocado tree.

I wasn't sure what was wrong with my keeper, but I knew that some days he moved very slowly as if every bone in his body hurt. Fortune-Teller wasn't very old. At least I don't think he was. None of the fur on his head had turned gray.

To kill time, Fortune-Teller took out a small vial and sprinkled a few drops of perfume on my head.

I whined and tried to twist out of his arms. "I hate perfume. It makes me sneeze."

"He hates perfume," the boy said. "It makes him sneeze."

Fortune-Teller didn't listen. He sprinkled on more.

I sneezed a giant sneeze.

Fortune-Teller looked up at the boy in wide-eyed wonder. "How did you know that?"

Uxmal shrugged. He picked up a clay pot and sang as he watered a flowerbed. He paused.

A gentle breeze rustled the blossoms.

He sang another line.

A stronger gust of wind stirred through the flowers. Their buds bobbed and swayed.

It was odd. All the nearby trees and shrubs remained completely still.

Uxmal sang, paused, then nodded and laughed. He sang again.

I listened in amazement. It sounded like he was having a conversation with the flowers. I jumped down from Fortune-Teller's lap and trotted over to him. "Are you talking to the plants?"

"Yes."

"Are they talking back?"

"They sure are."

"They've never talked to me."

Uxmal squatted in front of me. "Have you ever lifted a leg and watered them?"

I glanced away guiltily.

"Would you want to talk to someone who did that to you?"

A commotion began in the tangle of trees beyond the city wall, but this was not unusual. The people of Chilaam were locked in a constant battle with the jungle. Many dangers lurked in its thick undergrowth and spreading canopy. Sometimes a wild animal jumped the city wall and had to be driven out. Sometimes poisonous plants tried to slip into the city and take root.

The top of a nearby palm tree shook.

Uxmal tilted his head as if listening intently and slowly nodded.

"Is the palm tree talking to you?" I asked.

Uxmal motioned for me to be quiet. After a moment, he asked, "Did you understand what he told me?"

I shook my head. "All I heard was the wind."

"Palm said the monkeys and snakes have formed a new alliance called Jungle Liberation. They are tired of men living on their land. They have declared war on humans."

I crossed my paws and rested my chin on them. I wasn't surprised that the monkeys and snakes had joined forces. They had a lot in common. There were over fifty different types of snakes in the jungle, most of them poisonous, all of them dangerous. Monkeys were dangerous too—and *sneaky*. I recalled the first time I had ever seen one. When I was a pup, Fortune-Teller visited a friend who owned a monkey. He resembled a human, except he had more fur and a long tail. The little furry freak tormented me by pulling my ears and tail when the humans weren't watching. Every time I yelped in pain, he would immediately sit back and look innocent. A little later, he ran away and was never seen again.

The top of the palm tree shook again.

"Oh, that's not good," Uxmal muttered.

"What'd he say?" I asked.

"Jungle Liberation plans to kidnap a blue chihuahua and hold it for ransom."

"Why would they do that?" I asked.

"Probably to pay for the war. A sacred temple dog is worth a lot of cocoa beans. Keep your guard up, Kichi," Uxmal warned.

"I shall." Other cities had blue chihuahuas, but I was the only one in Chilaam.

He poured water over his hands and cleaned them with a rag. "I'm finished in the garden. Venerable Fortune-Teller, may I play fetch with Kichi?"

"You may." My keeper handed Uxmal my favorite toy, a short braided rope knotted on both ends. Under

Fortune-Teller's watchful gaze, Uxmal tossed it across the green and I chased after it. Playing with my friend was a lot of fun.

"Snake!" someone shrieked from the other side of the plaza.

"Where?" another voice yelled.

"In the cocoa tree grove!"

It was sheer pandemonium. Half the humans started running away from the cocoa tree grove while the other half rushed toward it to protect the precious pods growing there.

Suddenly, a monkey dropped from a palm and landed in front of me. He grabbed me, tucked me under his armpit, and scrambled up the tree.

No one noticed except Uxmal. "Drop that dog!" he screeched in Monkey and scurried up the tree after me.

The monkey bared his teeth and hissed over his shoulder.

Just then, a coconut loosened from the palm tree and conked him on the head.

Squealing in pain, he let me drop.

I felt myself tumble down, down, down. Fortunately, a hand shot out and grabbed my fur before I splatted on the ground.

"Gotcha!" Uxmal exclaimed. He scrambled down the trunk.

Fortune-Teller was waiting at the base of the tree. He snatched me from Uxmal and hugged me tight. "Oh, Sugar! You poor baby! Did that mean monkey hurt you?"

I trembled all over and snuggled deep into Fortune-Teller's comforting arms.

He turned to Uxmal. "Thank you so much! You deserve your freedom for what you've done. I'm going to speak to my brother right away."

Once I had calmed down, I realized what had happened. The snake in the grove was a mere distraction so the monkey could kidnap me. From now on, I'd have my guard up.

"Kernel, cob, and husk!" Ah Tok thundered as he strode toward us, fists clenched, face black with anger.

"What's wrong, brother?" Fortune-Teller asked.

"What's wrong? Everything! Two slaves escaped last night. The two most valuable of the whole lot! I was going to sell them to pay my debts." Ah Tok collapsed on the steps next to his brother. "I'm ruined!"

I knew Uxmal's chances for freedom were ruined as well. Any mercy Ah Tok might have shown him for rescuing me had vanished.

Chapter Three

The escaped slaves were never seen again, although Ah Tok and his soldiers searched the city, fields, and jungle.

I couldn't help but praise the gods when Ah Tok was bitten by a poisonous snake and carried home by his soldiers. Don't get me wrong. I didn't rejoice in Ah Tok's misery. But he moved into the Temple of the Two-Headed Snake so Fortune-Teller, his brother, could care for him. This meant that Uxmal came too.

Now I could see my best friend every day.

One evening, as Uxmal gave me a bath, he told me about his home. Face shining with pride, he talked about Tulum, a city perched on the edge of a great sea.

I listened carefully as he described the noise of waves pounding the shore and the feel of cool, salty breezes against the cheek. I had always lived in a steamy jungle and couldn't imagine standing at the edge of a body of water with no end.

"When you swim underwater," he said as he toweled me dry, "you can see fish of all colors. Bright blue. Brilliant yellow. Dazzling orange."

"What else do you remember?" I asked.

"Sitting on Tulum's eastern wall and looking down on the beach, a ribbon of pure white sand. At sunset, when the fishermen's canoes return, I watch them unload baskets of shrimp and lobster and crab." Uxmal suddenly grew very quiet. He began brushing my fur. "If only we could be who we really are and do what we really want to do."

Just then, a harsh noise sounded far away beyond the city walls.

The brush slid from Uxmal's hand.

"What was that?" I asked sleepily.

Uxmal straightened. "A conch shell."

I yawned. I didn't know what that was and was too tired to ask.

Uxmal placed me on my pillow and covered me with a cotton blanket.

Resting my head on my paws, I settled deeper into bed. Pleasant thoughts filled my mind. I dreamed I was chewing on a bone and drifted to sleep.

A frightful crash awoke me.

I could hear men fighting beyond the temple walls. The air was filled with screaming and yelling and weapons clashing together.

I shivered in fear.

Uxmal came running in. He scooped me up and tucked me close to his chest, so close that I could hear his heart pounding.

"What's going on?"

"The city's under attack. Everything will be all right," he assured me. He placed me inside a large wicker basket where we kept our dirty clothes until wash day and covered me with a damp towel. "You'll be safe here," he said, and then he ran off.

Listening to the attack on the temple, I trembled in fear. I knew that a city almost as grand as Chilaam lay to the west. Until recently, it had been Chilaam's chief trading partner but something had happened and it no longer exchanged goods with us.

Feet rushed past my hiding place. "Check every room," a man roared. "He must be here."

I felt a sneeze coming and laid my paws under my nose to stifle it. The least little noise would give me away.

Blue chihuahuas like me are considered sacred because we are rare. Enemies often try to steal a city's temple dog, its most powerful link to the gods.

The sounds of a struggle reached my ears. How I wished I could see what was happening.

After a long time, the temple grew quiet.

I pushed on the sides of the basket with my front paws and knocked it over, tumbling out.

Fortune-Teller and his brother lay on the stone floor. They had been gagged, blindfolded, and bound hand and foot. I breathed a sigh of relief to see their chests moving up and down. They had been knocked unconscious, but not killed.

I gnawed through their bonds, then ran to the room where Uxmal slept.

He was gone.

Chapter Four

My heart sank to my paws. The attackers had stolen Uxmal.

The city of Chilaam had just started Dead Time. Whoever took the boy must have known that no one would follow them, for anyone starting a journey during this time would be cursed by the gods and doomed to disaster.

That didn't apply to dogs. I headed toward the open door.

Halfway there, I stopped, torn between loyalty to Fortune-Teller and love for Uxmal. If I left, my faithful keeper would get in trouble. He would lose his job at the temple. Or worse. But someone had stolen Uxmal. The boy was in greater trouble.

I bolted outside and dodged around overturned baskets, broken spears and wounded men. It looked like no one would be going after my boy, at least not for a while. I had to do it myself. But I had never been outside the city. And the jungle held all kinds of dangers.

A guard was pushing the gate shut. Once it closed I would be trapped inside the city. Taking a deep breath, I dashed through. I don't think he saw me. The gate very nearly caught my tail.

Torches blazed from the city wall, illuminating heavy footprints in the dirt. They all headed away from Chilaam.

I followed them until they disappeared into the dark jungle. I stopped. Which way should I go? I was a little dog alone in a big jungle.

Tree branches to my right rustled. Something was approaching. I stared into the dark and hoped it wasn't something big and dangerous.

A few seconds later, a toucan popped out of the dark leaves. He landed on a low branch, ruffled his feathers, and peered down at me. "Why the long face, Sonny? You look like you just lost your best friend."

"I have. Did you see some humans pass by?"

"Just got here. Sorry."

"I was following footprints, but now I've lost the trail."

"Follow your nose," the toucan advised cheerfully. "The nose always knows."

Well, of course. Why didn't I think of that? I put my muzzle to the ground and found Uxmal's trail. It smelled wonderful—like incense with a touch of vanilla.

"Thank you!" I hurried off.

"You owe me a favor, Sonny!"

"Indeed I do," I yelled over my back.

There was no smell of fear in Uxmal's trail. That was puzzling. Taken the way he was in the dead of night, he must have been afraid.

His captors were heading due east, not west toward our rival city. That surprised me.

I ran until I could run no longer. Panting, I paused by a tree root to rest and do some quick figuring in my head. Those men were bigger than I was and took longer strides. I'd never catch up with them.

"Hello there, friend," a gravelly voice said from the leafy canopy above.

I jumped in surprise and searched for the source of the voice. First I looked left, then right, and finally up. I sneezed. Looking up always made me do that.

"I feel your pain, buddy. I've got allergies too. Stay right there and I'll send someone down with some medicine."

Before I could say Happy Dog Day, I found myself tucked in a great hairy arm, flying from branch to branch. Each swing took me further and further from the ground. I trembled in fear.

My transportation turned out to be a long-tailed monkey just like the one who tried to kidnap me earlier. Maybe it was the same monkey. I couldn't be sure.

He plopped me down in a tree house and grinned, showing very long and very sharp teeth. "I caught the temple dog!" he bragged as he pranced around, swinging his arms overhead. "I'm the smartest, richest, handsomest creature in the jungle!"

"And the most modest," said a monkey lounging in a hammock. It was the same gravelly voice I had heard earlier. He had a long curly tail and a big, red nose. It looked like he had bad allergies.

Monkeys of all colors, sizes, and shapes hovered around him. One was trimming his fur while another cut his toenails. A female monkey wearing a hat at a jaunty angle was picking lice from his head and popping them into his open mouth.

"Hi, there," the monkey in the hammock said to me. He held a drink in one hand, a cigar in the other. "Welcome! My name's Copal."

"Mine is Kichi."

"Get my friend here a drink," Copal said to the monkey picking lice.

She obeyed without hesitation and handed me a drink in a coconut cup.

I sniffed cautiously. It had an odd smell about it.

"Ah, come on, kid," Copal said. "Live a little. It's just coconut milk with a little rum."

I pushed it back. "I don't drink."

He took a long drag on his cigar. "And I don't inhale."

All the monkeys screeched in delight at his joke.

"Give my friend here whatever he wants."

"Water would be nice," I said.

Copal gestured toward a monkey. "You heard the dog."

A cup of water was placed in front of me. I sniffed it and took a cautious lick. I didn't taste anything suspicious. I peeped over the edge of the tree house as I drank. That was a giant mistake! My head began to swim. I couldn't even see the jungle floor. How was I going to get out of here? I looked frantically for an escape route, but didn't see one.

I recalled what the palm tree had told Uxmal. The monkeys and snakes planned to kidnap a temple dog. So far, I didn't see any snakes, but I definitely was the monkeys' prisoner.

A low moan, the sound of someone in pain, made me shiver. I looked around for its source, but all I saw were flat platforms in neighboring trees laden with gorgeous flowers. The moaning was coming from them.

About fifteen monkeys carrying flowers swung in on vines, dumped the plants wherever they could find an empty space, and swung away.

The moaning grew louder.

A vulture swooped in and landed on a branch opposite Copal. He hunched over and swiveled his head all about.

"Tell me good news," Copal said in his raspy voice.

"Ain't no more orchids in this part of the jungle. We've cleaned 'em out."

I jerked my head toward the flowers. Was that what they were? Orchids? I had never seen one before.

"Be on the lookout for toucans," the vulture said. "They've sided with the *humans*." He made the word sound dirty.

The shifty-eyed bird of prey gave me a bad feeling. He looked in my direction and wrinkled his brow as if he hadn't noticed me before. "Where'd the mangy mutt come from?"

I bristled. "First of all, I'm a chihuahua, not a mutt, and secondly, I don't have mange."

"Where'd you get this clown, Copal? Whadya do? Drag a cocoa bean down the trail to see what would come outta the jungle?"

"A cocoa bean down the trail!" Copal roared in laughter. "Where do you come up with these things?"

I didn't like this bird. He looked shifty and untrustworthy. Since he didn't have the common courtesy to tell me his name, I decided to call him Shifty.

The monkey wearing a hat searched through Copal's hair, paused like a jaguar stalking prey, then pounced.

"Oh please," a tiny voice yelled. "Don't eat me! Think of my ten thousand children."

The monkey popped the louse into Copal's open mouth.

He swallowed it right down. "Delicious. Pick me another one," he said lazily, rubbing his tummy. "See if you can get me a handful of those ten thousand children."

"Get rid of the pup," Shifty said, glaring at me. "It ain't natural for a chihuahua to be in the jungle. I don't trust anything that hangs out with humans."

Copal laughed and slapped me on the paw in a friendly kind of way. "Don't worry about anything he says, kid. He don't mean anything by it."

"Soon as the humans find their chihuahua missing," the vulture said, "they'll send someone out to look for him."

Copal nodded. "But they won't find him. Instead, they'll find a ransom note. Sea Gull is on his way here. I'll have him write it and deliver it. Chilaam will think a rival city stole their temple dog. It will start a war. The humans will destroy each other and everything will be ours again. No more pesky humans stealing whatever they want and plundering our jungle."

Worry sliced through me. Would I be the cause of war between two cities?

Just then, a boa slithered in.

Monkeys scattered, screeching in terror. The vulture flapped off as well, leaving Copal all alone.

The boa turned its cold blue eyes on me.

A chill coursed through me.

She inched forward.

I realized I was exactly the size of a tasty, nutritious snack for a snake her size. I backed up to the edge of the tree house.

There was no escape.

Chapter Five

"A chihuahua," the boa said, her eyes glittering in anger. "What's he doing here?" She lapped her coils around Copal.

"You're strangling me, Babe."

"No, *this* is strangling." She tightened the coils.

"Relax, Babe. You're getting all uptight."

The coils tightened a bit more. "I get uptight when someone betrays me. Having a dog here means you're secretly working with humans."

"Aw, come on, Babe," the monkey choked out. "You know me better than that. I kidnapped him. He's part of my plan to start a war between the humans. Once they're gone, the jungle will be ours again." His voice turned velvety. "And we will rule it together, Babe. Just you and me."

The coils loosened. Her gaze softened.

I rolled my eyes. How disappointing. I thought snakes were smarter than that. Imagine her swallowing that line! But then again, snakes swallowed lots of things. Rats, rabbits, and little dogs like me! I definitely needed to keep a sharp eye on her.

Suddenly, the air was filled with the sound of hundreds of wings beating together.

Copal jerked his head around. "Run! It's a raid!" He grabbed a vine and swung away.

An army of parrots, dragonflies and butterflies swooped toward the platform. Some landed in nearby trees. Others perched on branches. Still others fluttered onto the tree house itself.

A large spotted jaguar, accompanied by several smaller black ones, leaped into the center of the tree house. A toucan set down beside him.

"The orchids are secured!" a dragonfly announced from a distant tree. "They are unharmed."

"Good work, Air Force," the jaguar said.

A big blue butterfly flew in and hovered in front of him. "The trees are empty. They've fled. All clear, except for a snake and a dog." She spoke in a honeyed voice. All butterflies have kind, soft voices, but hers was particularly sweet.

"Go after Copal and his gang," the jaguar ordered.

Parrots, dragonflies, and butterflies obeyed without question.

Squinting, the toucan turned toward Babe the Boa. "We've got the goods on you two. When we catch Copal, he's going away for a long time."

She sat in a clump of coils, watching with cold disinterest. "I don't know a thing. My hands are clean."

"Madam," the toucan said, "you don't have hands." He turned toward me. "I must say I'm surprised to see you here, Sonny. You and the snake make an unlikely pair."

All at once, I recognized the bird. "You're the toucan I met earlier."

"That is correct. Would you explain to me how a chihuahua manages to climb a tree?"

"I didn't. I was walking through the jungle when a monkey grabbed me and whisked me up here."

The jaguar frowned at me. "I knew they were kidnapping orchids. I didn't know they had worked their way up to dogs."

"Copal and his gang are a bad lot," the toucan said.

The jaguar nodded in agreement. "First, flowernapping, now dognapping." He circled the boa. "Babe, you really stepped in it this time. You're under arrest."

"It's Princess Babe to you. I'm royalty. You can't arrest me."

The jaguar put his face very close to hers. "I just did. No one is above the law. Not even you." He addressed the jaguar to his left. "Take her away."

One of the jaguars turned and snapped out orders to the rest. "You heard Lord Jaguar. Secure the snake, but watch the coils. She can have 'em around your neck before you know it."

A jaguar clamped his jaws across the back of her head while the others stretched her out straight. Spacing themselves evenly along her back, they picked her up in their mouths. They heaved her long body to the edge of the tree house and unceremoniously rolled her over.

She landed with a bone-jarring thud.

I cringed. "Oooh, that's gotta hurt."

"Don't waste your sympathy," Lord Jaguar said. "She's pure evil."

"I hope she didn't squash anything when she landed," the toucan remarked.

Lord Jaguar squinted at the ground. "I guess it's true what they say. The snake doesn't fall far from the tree."

"Uh," the toucan said, scratching his nose in embarrassment, "that's *the apple*. The apple doesn't fall far from the tree."

Lord Jaguar gave him a lopsided grin. "Yeah, but in this case, it was a snake."

The other jaguars scrambled down the tree trunks and had the boa in their mouths before she came to.

"Let's get your feet back on the ground," Lord Jaguar said to me. His eyes twinkled charmingly. He spoke slowly, as if choosing his words wisely. He gave off a special honey scent that reminded me of Fortune-Teller. It made me trust him immediately.

He eased his mouth around me and carried me down the tree as gingerly as if I were one of his kittens, then set me on the ground. "I'd like to help you get home, kid, but I need every paw and talon I've got. We've got to take the orchids back."

"I understand. Anyway, I'm not going home until I find my boy."

"I strongly urge you to get out of the jungle," Lord Jaguar said.

"I have to find Uxmal."

"The jungle's a dangerous place full of evildoers," he said. "You'll be safer in your temple."

"How did you know I was a temple dog?"

"That blue fur is a dead giveaway, kid. And there's a rumor in the jungle that Chilaam's sacred temple dog is missing. Goes by the name Kichi."

"That would be me," I admitted.

"That's not the only jungle rumor," the toucan said, his face suddenly sad. "There's talk of war. The Emperor of Chilaam has vowed to follow the men who attacked his city. He plans to send out an army as soon as Dead Time is over."

"Oh, no," I said in disbelief. It was bad enough that Uxmal had been taken. Now I worried that he might be recaptured by Ah Tok. Or killed in battle. I had to find him before that happened.

Chapter Six

I sniffed around until I picked up Uxmal's scent and trotted off.

The people who had taken him were still heading due east. I found that odd. Chilaam's greatest rival lay to the north. Why would these people head east?

"Wait for us, kid," Lord Jaguar called out.

To my surprise, he loped up beside me. The toucan held on tight to his shoulder fur and stretched out his wings for balance.

"It looks like you're heading east," the jaguar said. "We just happen to be heading in that direction too."

"That's quite a coincidence," I said.

Lord Jaguar raised his right paw. "Honest Jaguar. My den is east of here." He pointed vaguely ahead of us.

As it turned out, Lord Jaguar was a talkative fellow and likable as well. I expected the lord of the jungle to be an arrogant snob, but the old saying proved true: You can't judge a turtle by its shell.

"Copal used to be king of Animalot," Lord Jaguar said. "He got kicked out for corruption, bribery, you name it. Just an all around shady character. He probably recognized you as a temple dog and knew you were worth a lot of cocoa beans. You might want to dye that fur the first chance you get."

"Good idea," I said.

"Me and my forces are trying to make the jungle safe for everyone, but we have a lot of hard work ahead of us. Most plants and animals are kind and peace-loving. If you leave them alone, they'll leave you alone. Some even go out of their way to be helpful — like King Tulum of Xochitl. He leaves leftovers in the jungle for us."

The toucan cleared his throat. "Ummmmm...That's King *Xochitl* of *Tulum*."

"Oh, right." Lord Jaguar gave an embarrassed laugh. "I always get that backwards.

"Tulum?" I brightened at the name. "That's where Uxmal is from!"

"Uxmal...Uxmal..." Lord Jaguar rolled the name around in his mouth. "What an odd name." He looked over his shoulder at the toucan. "Do you remember a boy named Uxmal?"

"No."

"Neither do I. Are you sure the name was 'Uxmal?'" Lord Jaguar asked.

"Positive."

"I know every human in Tulum, from the potter to the king himself. There's no one by that name."

"That's odd," I said.

We walked on in silence.

"Tell me about Tulum." I wanted to learn everything I could about my boy's city.

The toucan spoke first. He described it in detail as only a toucan can—from a bird's eye view.

Lord Jaguar took a more practical approach. "Tulum is one of Chilaam's trading partners. It sells seashells, honey, and dried fish to other cities in return for cocoa beans, orchids, and other things it needs."

"The cocoa bean trade I understand. I often went to market with Fortune-Teller. A rabbit cost ten cocoa beans. A pumpkin cost four. But I don't remember anyone selling orchids. Why would anyone want them?"

"The humans of Tulum use them as medicine," Lord Jaguar said. "And orchids only grow in the jungle, so the king sends people out from time to time to harvest them."

"Is that why Copal had collected all the orchids? To keep humans from picking them?"

"Yes. Copal believes humans are evil and should be kept out of the jungle."

"What do you believe?"

"I believe in peaceful co-existence. Man can live in harmony with all plants and animals as long as there is no wanton destruction of the jungle."

"What does wanton destruction mean?"

He tapped his paw against his muzzle in deep thought. "It means destroying things just because you feel like it. Humans should only take what they need."

"And they need orchids?"

"Yes. They use the roots to make a nutritious drink that's good for the bones."

"I wonder if it would help Fortune-Teller. He has something wrong with his bones."

"I'm sure it would," Lord Jaguar said. "It helped my mother. That's why she lives in Tulum. For the medicine."

"The humans let a man-eating jaguar live among them?" I blurted. As soon as the words were out, I wished I could grab them and stuff them back in my mouth. Lots of animals lived in Chilaam, but none of them ate man.

Lord Jaguar smiled indulgently. "We don't eat humans. That's just a vicious rumor. They're too tough and stringy." His eyes crinkled in amusement. "Or so I've been told."

"Tell Kichi the story of your mother and the King of Tulum," the toucan prompted. He still clung to Lord Jaguar's fur, trying desperately to keep his balance.

"Yes, please," I said. "I love stories. Especially ones with happy endings."

"One beautiful spring morning," Lord Jaguar began, "my mother went out hunting. She heard a squalling sound and thought it was a hungry cub. She followed it and found that it wasn't a jaguar at all."

"What was it?"

"A human baby."

"Where was its mother?"

"Dead. Bandits had attacked a band of travelers and killed everyone."

"How sad."

"Yes, but the story has a happy ending. Mother found the baby hidden in a hollow log, took it back to the den, and raised it with me and my brother. The baby learned Jaguar and other animal languages. To Mother's dismay, one day he pushed up from the ground and started to walk on his hind paws. From then on, Mother called him Hind Paws.

"A long time went by. After a while, Mother couldn't hunt any more because her bones ached too much. My brothers and I took turns bringing her food. One day, Hind Paws went out and didn't come back. Mother was worried sick. She insisted upon looking for him, even though she was in great pain. We followed him to a spot where his tracks met human footprints. He joined them. We trailed them to Tulum.

"Mother sat there all day, watching. The moon set and the sun rose and still my mother stared at the city walls. After a long time, she said, 'He has gone back to his people and forgotten us.' We returned home."

"You said this story had a happy ending," I complained.

"Keep your feathers on," the toucan scolded. "Lord Jaguar isn't finished yet."

"One day, not very much later, Hind Paws returned to the den. He brought men with him."

"This still sounds like a sad story," I said in alarm.

Lord Jaguar ignored me. "They had a stretcher with them. Hind Paws told Mother that he wanted to take her to Tulum where they had miracle medicine that could help her bone problem." Lord Jaguar grew quiet for a moment. "She went with him and lives there still. Hind Paws was right. The medicine didn't cure her, but it makes her bones stop hurting for a while."

"It does have a happy ending!" I said in relief. "But where does the King of Tulum come into the story?"

"Oh, yeah, right," Lord Jaguar said with an embarrassed laugh. "I left out that part. The baby she saved was the first-born son of the King of Tulum. He's now king."

The jungle undergrowth parted and a jaguar with sleek black fur ambled toward us. She had the most unusual eyes. They slanted up slightly and were as blue as a cloudless sky.

"This is my wife," Lord Jaguar said, taking her paw in his. "Lady Jaguar, this is Kichi."

"It's a pleasure to meet you," she said in a soft voice. "Husband, the parrots report a disturbance in the jungle. Pods are being stolen from cocoa trees. It appears monkeys took them."

Lord Jaguar wrinkled his brow fiercely. "Are you sure it was monkeys and not humans?"

"Monkey fur was found in the tree branches."

"Tell Special Forces to meet me at the sink hole." Lord Jaguar spoke to me. "It looks like this is where we part company, kid."

I nodded. "Thank you for your help."

The toucan reached into his feathers and pulled out a wooden whistle on a string. He smiled like a bird with a secret. "If you find yourself in trouble, blow on this."

I thanked him, took it, and hung it around my neck. I turned to Lord Jaguar's wife. "It was a pleasure meeting you."

"I hope we meet again some day," she said. "Until then, may your path be pebble-free."

I waved good-bye and walked away.

"Hey, kid!" Lord Jaguar said. "When you come to a fork in the road, take it."

Puzzling over Lord Jaguar's remark, I glanced over my shoulder.

He just flashed his usual lopsided grin.

Chapter Seven

I traveled on and on. My stomach ached from hunger. There was probably food all around me in the thick jungle undergrowth, but I had never hunted in my life and had no idea how to do it. I didn't dare eat unknown plants. What if they were poisonous? How was a dog to know?

Gone were the comforts to which I was so long accustomed. How I missed Fortune-Teller. He took such good care of me. Sometimes he gave me a bone to gnaw. Sometimes he gave me a good soapy bath. Afterwards, I would lie on my back in his lap while he trimmed my whiskers and the long hair over my eyes, inside my ears, and on my stomach.

The fragrant aroma of flowers filled the air and made me lose Uxmal's trail. Long stemmed flowers danced in the breeze.

Nose to the ground, I veered to the left and sniffed about.

Nothing.

Heading to the right produced the same result.

Nothing!

Uxmal's scent was gone!

I was deep in the jungle and completely lost. As if that weren't bad enough, it was growing dark.

Through a lush tangle of greenery, I spied a Mayan home topped with a thatched roof. It had a door but no windows and would give me shelter for the night.

Encouraged by the sight, I trotted forward. Maybe the people who lived here would be nice. Maybe they had seen Uxmal and his captors pass by. I poked my head inside and looked around.

"Help me!" a sweet voice called out. "Oh, help me, please."

The plea came from a high corner. There, trapped in a spider's web, was the most beautiful butterfly I had ever seen. It was bright blue—a true blue, not blue-gray like me.

"Go away, pup," a high-pitched voice said, "unless ya want to be my next meal!" A gigantic spider clinging to its equally gigantic web took a menacing step forward. The web bounced.

My heart thumped and I began to tremble. We chihuahuas are not known for our courage.

The spider dropped in front of my face. It dangled by a long slender thread. "Boo!"

I bolted out the door.

"Oh, please come back," the butterfly begged.

The spider cackled in victory.

I sped away from the hut. Part of me said, "It was probably poisonous." Another part answered, "You're afraid of a little spider." Deeply ashamed of myself, I stopped running.

How could I ever take another drink of water and look at my reflection without seeing a coward?

I searched for a tree branch, something not too heavy for a little dog, but long enough to reach the spider web. I tested one, but it was too big. A second one was too small. The third was just right.

I dragged it toward the hut and dropped it at the door. I peeped inside to see where the spider was.

She sat smugly by the trapped butterfly.

Grabbing the tree branch in my mouth, I dragged it inside.

"Whatcha up to, pup?" the spider cried out in alarm.

"A little wanton destruction," I replied. Standing on my hind legs with the branch in my mouth, I swiped at the web.

"Ha, ha, ya missed me!" the spider said.

I swung again.

"Not even close!" The spider laughed. "Oooooh, I'm afraid of the big bad dog."

The next blow split the web in half.

Off flew the butterfly. "Thank you, Mr. Dog!"

"It took me forever to build that web!" the spider screeched. "Forever!"

I followed the blue butterfly out the door.

She lit on a tree branch beyond my reach and fluttered her wings. "My, that was close! How can I ever repay you?"

"No need. I'm glad to help."

She dipped her wings in gratitude. "You are very brave."

I tilted my head, trying to recall where I had heard that honeyed voice before. "You were with Lord Jaguar when he rescued me from Copal's gang!"

She smiled. "Yes. And now you've returned the favor by rescuing *me*." She fluttered to the tip of my nose and gave me a butterfly kiss. "Thank you."

My heart nearly fell to the tip of my tail. She stayed on my nose and I had to look cross-eyed to focus on her.

Suddenly, her wings stopped moving. "Listen."

I heard it too. My ears shot up at the sound of distant voices.

"Y'all be careful now, ya hear?" someone said. "The jungle is lousy with Lord Jaguar's patrols."

I knew that voice. It belonged to Shifty the Vulture.

The butterfly and I hid behind a clump of bushes.

Three monkeys carrying bags on their backs swung through the trees.

"I'm going in for a closer look," the blue butterfly said.

"You can't," I protested. "It's dangerous."

"I know what I'm doing." She took off, skimming over flowers and bushes.

"Wait for me," I whispered, not at all sure I was doing the right thing.

Chapter Eight

I sneaked up on Shifty and his monkeys and hid behind a tree. From this angle I could see what they were doing, but it didn't make any sense.

They circled a fire. The smell of hot glue wafted from a pot hanging over it. Each monkey emptied his bag in front of him. Out spilled cocoa pods. Under Shifty's supervision, they split them open with their fingernails, scooped out the beans, and put them back into the bags. Then they filled the cocoa pods with sand. Next, they dipped a paint brush into the pot and carefully sealed each cocoa pod shut. They blew on the glue to make it dry faster.

One thing was certain. Whatever they were doing had to be underhanded or illegal or both if Shifty was involved.

Wings fluttered behind me. I jumped, then relaxed when I saw it was the blue butterfly.

Shifty stiffened. "Did ya hear something?" he asked the monkeys.

One of them scratched an armpit, found a louse, and ate it. The others kept working.

"There it is again," Shifty said. He glanced left, right, and over his shoulder.

"It's just your imagination, Boss," a monkey said.

"Can't be that," said a second one. "He ain't got one."

"He ain't got what?" asked a third as he lazily painted a pod shut.

"An imagination."

"What's an eeee-mag-uh-na-shun?" asked Monkey 3.

"It sounds like a disease," said Monkey 4.

"Will you morons shut up!" Shifty screamed. "I can't hear."

"*Humpft!*" said Monkey 3. "Whatever he's got, it sure makes you mean as a sore-tailed monkey."

Shifty turned and hopped toward the clump of trees where we hid. He tilted his head as if he were listening carefully.

I stayed as still as possible. The blue butterfly lit on a nearby leaf and remained unmoving.

"We're done, Boss," one of the monkeys called.

Shifty scanned the jungle one last time and hopped back to the monkeys. "Next step is to put the fake pods on the bottom of each bag like so." He gingerly put one in. "Then, when the bag's half full, start using the good pods."

"Why don't we fill it all with fake pods, Boss?" asked Monkey 3.

Shifty slapped him upside the head with his wing. "Because the inspector checks the pods at the top, but not the pods at the bottom."

"He don't?"

"He don't." Shifty beat his wings together. "Everybody! Let's go!"

Nothing happened.

Shifty, clearly annoyed, yelled, "All monkeys! Now!"

Monkeys dropped from the trees like a slow rain. They rubbed sleep from their eyes.

Shifty eyed them in disgust. "And to think I'm looking at the top bananas of monkey society."

"Bananas?" Monkey 2 asked, looking all around. "Where? I'm real hungry."

"Me too," said another monkey.

"I don't see no bananas," said Monkey 1. He pushed Monkey 2. "You ate up all the bananas, didn't you?"

Monkeys 1 and 2 began rolling around in the dirt, clawing, biting, and shrieking.

Shifty flapped toward them and used his sharp talons to separate the two. Then, he gave the monkeys some final instructions. "Take the pods to Sea Gull. Go directly to the palm grove. Do not pick any coconuts. Do not stop for bananas."

The monkeys exchanged glances and grumbled.

Shifty shook his head. "I gotta have a long talk with Copal some day about the company he keeps."

Monkeys hefted bags of sand-filled cocoa pods over their shoulders and scurried away.

By firelight I could barely make out the emblem painted on each bag. It showed a quetzal, the sacred bird of the jungle and the symbol of Chilaam. Quetzals had long tail feathers of vivid green. Only the emperor of Chilaam was allowed to wear clothing made from them. A warrior could receive no higher honor than for the emperor to reward him with a sack of feathers.

The blue butterfly and I remained hidden until everyone left.

She fluttered over to me. "Lord Jaguar needs to know immediately that Copal's gang is tampering with cocoa pods. If only I knew where he was right now."

"He's at the sink hole."

"How do you know that?"

"I was with Lord Jaguar when he received word that monkeys had been stealing cocoa pods from the trees. He headed there to meet Special Forces."

"Thank you for that information!" She started to fly away.

"Wait! Tell him about the quetzals on the bags."

She hovered. "Do you think that's important?"

"Yes, but I'm not sure why."

"I'll tell him." She curled her antennae to signal a fond good-bye and left.

I walked east until the jungle darkened and night crept over it. The thick canopy of trees made it difficult to see the stars. I couldn't tell which way I was going.

Luckily, I found a hollow log. After making sure it had no occupants, I crept inside and curled into a ball. I thought about home and Fortune-Teller. Back in Chilaam, I often searched for a sunny spot to nap because I loved the warmth of the sun. Fortune-Teller would scratch my tummy.

Thinking such pleasant thoughts, I fell asleep, even though my stomach ached with hunger.

Chapter Nine

I awoke at dawn to find a brown furry animal curled up beside me. It was about my size and had a long tail wrapped around it.

I decided in the best interest of my health to leave before it woke up. Trying not to disturb the thing, I slowly moved one paw and then the next.

It woke up, yawned, and unrolled a tongue at least five inches long. It had really sharp teeth, too. I froze and watched it stretch, scratch, and begin to groom itself. The thing turned enormous eyes, half the size of its face, on me and said, "How do you do? Who are you?"

"I'm Kichi. What are you?"

"I'm a kinkajou. The name's Fou Fou. Pleased to meet you."

"What are you doing here?"

"Let me make this clear. I came here out of fear. Some bad dudes are very near."

"Do you always talk in rhyme?"

"Every single time."

"That doesn't make sense."

"That's because you're dense."

I was annoyed by this fellow. His rhymes nearly made me bellow. Oh, no, I thought. He's making me *think* in rhyme. I crawled out of the hollow log.

Fou Fou the Kinkajou followed me.

"I must be on my way," I said.

"Where to on such a beautiful day?"

"I'm not certain. I'm looking for a boy."

"Black hair, not furry? With men in a hurry?"

"Yes! Where did they go?"

"How should I know?"

"But you saw men in a hurry?"

"My vision was blurry, but indeed they did scurry."

He led me to a cold campsite.

It had rained overnight and the ground was soggy. Mud squished between my toes. Men's water-filled tracks covered the ground. Most were enormous, but one set was much smaller than the rest.

I knew it had to be Uxmal's even though the rain had washed away his scent. I said good-bye to Fou Fou and raced away.

I heard him yell: "Hail and farewell! Follow that trail!"

All day I did just that. Finding water was no problem. I just drank out of puddles. As disgusting as it was, it beat being thirsty. But I was still terribly hungry and needed to find food.

After a while, the ground dried and the tracks disappeared, but I picked up Uxmal's scent. The men with him left the odor of fish and salt.

As I traveled through the jungle, I paid close attention to stray sounds. I had escaped twice from the monkeys and had no desire to be in their clutches again. The jungle was usually a noisy place with birds chattering in the canopy and bees buzzing from flower to flower. Now it had fallen quiet, as if every living being was holding its breath.

"Ki...chi." A deep voice broke the silence.

I froze.

"Ki...chi."

Searching for the source of the voice, I glanced around. Was it the wind? Or did someone say my name?

"Ki...chi." The voice sounded wooden.

"Good grief!" a second voice boomed. "The monkeys will catch him by the time you get his attention. Kichi! Hide in the ferns! Now!"

Startled by the harsh order, I burrowed into the nearest bank of ferns. When I peeked out, I saw the most amazing thing.

A sapling growing on the side of the trail bent over and rubbed one of its branches across the ground. He was erasing my paw prints!

Monkeys gibbered. A moment later, they whooshed overhead, swinging on grapevines. Their chatter faded as they sped away.

Assuming that it was safe to come out, I poked out my nose.

"Not yet," the mysterious voice commanded.

I wiggled back in.

Shortly, another group of monkeys walking on their knuckles came down the trail. Some carried big clubs while others had long sticks. They thrashed

about, beating the bushes and poking through the thick undergrowth.

One of them pulled a vine out by its roots and shook it so hard its pods rattled. "Have you seen a little dog?"

I listened in amazement. The monkey wasn't speaking in his native tongue. It must have been Plant. Yet I understood every word. How was that possible?

The monkey twisted the vine until it nearly snapped in two pieces. "Have you seen him?"

"Yes," the vine gasped out. "Several days ago, a blue chihuahua named Kichi passed this way with twenty or so humans."

"Which way did he go?"

"South. I overheard them saying they were going to Nakbé."

The monkey cursed. He and his companions rushed off.

I had heard of that city before. Fortune-Teller often bought cotton cloth from its merchants.

I crept out of the fern bank, went over to the vine and licked it. When it didn't move, I assumed it was dead. A feeling of deep sadness filled me. I picked it up in my mouth and took it to the tree it had once climbed. I dug a hole, placed the roots inside, and tamped dirt around them.

"Thanks!" a cheerful voice said. "I needed that."

I jumped in surprise. I looked left and right, but I didn't see anyone.

"Yo, Sparky. It's me. Vinnie the Vine. Right here in front of you."

"Oh, hello."

The vine slowly inched up the tree trunk, muttering, "I save his miserable life and all he can say is 'oh, hello.' How about saying thank you?"

"Thank you," I said. "I'm sorry if I was rude. It's just that I'm surprised I can understand your language."

"Understand it?" Vinnie the Vine said. "You're speaking it like you were a born weed! Hey look! Your paws are already growing leaves."

I studied my paws.

"Gee, Sparky," Vinnie said. "It was a joke."

"Be...nice...to...him," the deep, wooden voice said.

I looked about to see who was talking.

"Look...up."

My gaze climbed from root to trunk to branches and leaves. All I saw was greenery. "Who's there?"

"You're...looking...straight...at...me. My...name...is...Mahogany."

"A tree is talking to me." I sat on my haunches in dismay.

"Well, sure!" Vinnie said as he crept up the tree trunk. "Animals talk all the time. Why wouldn't a tree?"

Mahogany chuckled. "Careful...Vinnie. I'm ticklish...around...that...knothole."

"I'm confused," I said.

"Why break with tradition?" Vinnie asked.

I ignored his sarcastic remark. "How come I can understand you now when I couldn't before?"

"Plants don't usually talk to passersby," Vinnie explained. "We made an exception with you because you helped a friend of ours."

"I did?"

"Blue Butterfly told us how you rescued her," Vinnie said. "That's why we saved you from the monkeys. Butterflies are our friends. They pollinate our flowers. Anyone who helps a friend is a friend of ours."

"He looks like a hungry friend to me," a kind voice said from the banana tree. "Here. Catch this."

A banana landed at my feet.

"Thank you." I peeled it and swallowed it in two giant gulps.

Another banana fell.

I gobbled it down as well. "There's something I don't understand."

"Sheesh!" Vinnie exclaimed. "Why am I not surprised?"

"The monkey was mean to you," I pointed out, "but still you spoke to him in Plant."

"Of course I did. He knows our language because he was raised in the jungle."

I thought about Uxmal. He was fluent in Plant. Did that mean he had spent a lot of time in the jungle? "I'm sorry to eat and run, but I have to go. It was nice meeting all of you."

"The pleasure was ours," all the plants along the trail crooned.

I sniffed the ground. Separating Uxmal's sweet smell from the odor of wet monkey proved easy. I followed it all day.

It was a pleasant walk. Wind rustled the leaves. The sun punched holes of light through the jungle's thick canopy.

At dusk, I left the path to look for a safe place to sleep.

A cluster of wildflowers invited me to spend the night with them. Apparently, my fame had spread. Every plant now knew the story of me and Blue Butterfly.

I snuggled into a lush tangle of greenery.

The wildflowers sang me to sleep.

By first light, I awoke. This time, I hadn't picked up any unexpected sleep partners. I left my bed, thanked everyone for their hospitality, and shook myself from head to toe. I was covered in muck, decaying leaves, and stray petals. I started to clean myself, but suddenly stopped. What was I thinking? This was perfect. No one would recognize me as a blue chihuahua looking like this.

I continued on. A new odor rode the breeze. It smelled salty, like the men who had taken Uxmal.

Suddenly, I emerged from the jungle and found my paws sinking into an unusually fine white dirt. I examined the grit between my toes. "This must be sand!" I exclaimed, recalling Uxmal's description of the beach around Tulum.

Straight ahead stretched an endless expanse of clear blue water.

"And that must be the sea!" I yelled, overjoyed.

My joy soon turned to deepest despair. Uxmal's trail went down the beach and disappeared into the water.

Chapter Ten

This was more than I could bear. It felt like my insides were collapsing. Completely forlorn, I sat by the seashore and watched waves crash against the shoreline. "Ux...mal!" I lifted my muzzle skyward and howled. "Ux...mal!"

"Oh, goodness gracious me," a female voice said. "Could you possibly make more noise?" A bright blue lobster was scuttling backwards toward the sea.

"Please don't go!" I begged. "I need to talk to someone."

"If I stay," the lobster said, waving a claw dramatically, "that outrageous screeching simply *must* stop. I will tolerate it no further. And stop that slouching."

I gulped down my next howl and forced myself to sit up straight. "How's that?" I asked in the quietest voice I could find.

"Much better." She went back to her business—scampering from rock to rock, grabbing them in her pincers and turning them over.

I followed her along the shoreline. "What are you doing?"

"Turning the rocks so they can get an even tan." That done, she picked up a coconut and started to whittle it with a sharpened sea shell.

I sat on my haunches and watched. "What are you doing now?"

"I'm having a dinner party. Nothing makes guests feel more special than a hand-carved coconut name plate."

"Why do they need that?"

"So they'll know where to sit."

"Isn't that an awful lot of work? Wouldn't it be easier to let them sit wherever they want?"

She looked stunned, as if she hadn't considered that possibility. She appeared gracious and kind, but not too bright.

A cloud drifted over the sun and sent a shadow over the sea, darkening it. I rubbed a paw across my forehead and sighed. Where could Uxmal have gone?

"It looks like you have a headache. You know, orange slices on your forehead will chase it away."

"No, it will only get juice in my eyes and make them sting. A headache's not my problem. Finding Uxmal is. Did you happen to see some people pass through here?"

"No. I've been busy preparing for my dinner party. Perhaps you should ask a sea gull."

I gulped. The mere mention of a sea gull sent a shiver through me. Copal, the monkey who kidnapped me, had said one of them would write the ransom note. And later, Shifty the Vulture had told the monkeys to take the fake cocoa pods to a sea gull. Whatever was afoot, sea gulls were involved. But having never met one, I had no idea what they looked like. "Where can I find one?"

"Just look around. You're surrounded by hundreds of them."

I ducked my head. "Where?"

"Over there, sweetheart," she said in a voice that suggested I wasn't the brightest puppy in the litter. She waved a claw toward a pile of sea-worn rock and driftwood covered with white birds with gray wings.

"Those are sea gulls?"

"In the feather!"

"And that big gray bird with the long beak?"

"That's a pelican."

Surrounded by sea gulls, the pelican looked like an emperor holding court. The scene reminded me of the many times Fortune-Teller had taken me to the palace for ceremonies.

The sea gulls sat unmoving, as if waiting for instructions.

Should I ask them about Uxmal? Could I trust them? I had no other options. I built up my courage and walked forward.

Chapter Eleven

Halfway to the sea gulls, my courage left me. But before I could turn around, the gulls took to the sky. Even the pelican flew off.

Why, they were more afraid of me than I was of them! Wings spread, they hovered overhead as if held up by an invisible force. From where I sat, it looked like magic.

One gull, braver than the rest, glided in, landed nearby, and folded his wings.

How graceful sea gulls were! How elegant! What marvelous creatures!

"Youse gotta reason for being on da beach?" he squawked.

The instant he opened his beak, he shattered all my illusions. Elegant, my front paw!

"Yes, I'm looking for a boy."

"Youse get off my beach," the gull screeched.

"I wasn't aware this beach belonged to you."

"This is Gull Alley. My mama was raised on dis beach. So was Pop. We been here since forever and don't you forget it."

"Look. I don't want any trouble. I just want some information."

"Information? That's gonna cost ya."

"I don't have any cocoa beans."

"Me and de boys don't eat *cocoa beans*. We're partial to fish."

A gull swooped in and landed next to him. "Hey, X-Rod. Who dat youse speaking wid?"

"A client. Now shut yer beak and let me do bidness." He directed his attention to me. "What you want me and de boys to do?"

"Nothing. I just want to know if you've seen a boy."

The gulls hovering overhead had apparently been eavesdropping. They sailed in for a landing, surrounding me.

I glanced around and my sense of fear deepened. I was trapped. I could only hope they weren't dog-eating sea gulls.

"Who you looking for, honey?" The question came from a female gull with a nasal, high-pitched voice that set my teeth on edge.

"I'm looking for a boy named Uxmal. His footprints went into the sea."

X-Rod pushed her aside. "Why you asking? Who youse guys working for?"

My dislike of this bird was growing by the second. "Youse guys?" I asked in a mocking tone. "Do you see more than one of me?"

"Don't you get smart wid me or I'll have to beat ya up."

"What are you going to do? Wing me to death?"

The gulls snickered.

"Shut up!" X-Rod said, glaring at his fellow gulls. He twisted toward me. "I won't use my wings. I'll peck your eyes out."

A vision of having no vision flashed through my mind. But I wasn't going to let him bully me. I lifted my chin. "I have very sharp teeth. See?" I bared them.

A girl gull wrapped a wing around X-Rod. "Sweetie, lighten up. He's just a little dog looking for his lost boy. Honey," she said, addressing me, "some people—"

"Shut up, Goldie," X-Rod scolded. "He could be working for the enemy."

"I'm just a dog looking for his best friend," I growled.

"Prove it." X-Rod took several menacing steps toward me.

My mind went blank. Then I recalled the whistle the toucan had given me. It was hidden under the layer of leaves and mud matting my coat. He had told me to blow it if I was ever in trouble. Now seemed like a good time. I scratched the whistle loose and blew as hard as I could.

The gulls covered their ears with their wings.

Goldie let out a happy squawk. "He's one of us!"

"Forgive me, Lord Chihuahua," X-Rod said, putting a wing to his breast and giving me a deep bow. "I meant no disrespect."

I couldn't help noticing that his tough-guy accent had magically disappeared.

All the gulls with him followed his lead and bowed.

My face must have reflected utter confusion. "Why the sudden change of heart?"

"Anyone who wears King Xochitl's whistle deserves my respect and assistance. I am Captain X-Rod of Lord Jaguar's Coast Guard and I beg your forgiveness for my earlier performance. Pretending to be a beach bully often works to my benefit. How may I be of service?"

It took me a moment to adjust to X-Rod's sudden turn around. "I am looking for a boy."

"You said that already," X-Rod said, with a small smile.

"Did you see him?"

"Yes, Lord Chihuahua."

"I don't like that name. Just call me Kichi."

Every gull within hearing let out a small gasp. They stood with their beaks hanging open, muttering "Kichi. Kichi."

"You are he. He is you!" Goldie babbled as she waddled forward. "King Xochitl said he misses you so much."

"I don't know anyone by that name."

"Yes! You do!" Goldie exclaimed. "King Xochitl said the two of you were good friends."

"That's right," X-Rod said. "Just before he climbed into the canoe, he said there was only one good thing about being held captive in Chilaam—meeting a wonderful dog named Kichi."

I felt faint. I suddenly understood that Uxmal was King Xochitl of Tulum.

Chapter Twelve

I sat on my haunches and digested that information. Apparently, King Xochitl and his men had used the fake name *Uxmal* so Ah Tok wouldn't know he had captured a king. That trick had saved Uxmal's life. The emperor would have sacrificed a captured king to the gods.

How silly I felt. The men who attacked Chilaam and took Uxmal were from Tulum. They were a rescue party! And now I understood why they had headed due east and why Uxmal's scent had held no fear. That route took them directly to the beach and their waiting canoes.

My whole trip had been useless. The boy I thought was my best friend had stuffed me in a basket of dirty laundry and left me without even saying good-bye. I felt like bawling. A tear slid from the corner of my eye. "Maybe I should just go home. I miss Fortune-Teller."

"But you've come so far," X-Rod said. "I'm sure King Xochitl would welcome a visit."

"I don't have a canoe and I can't swim."

"You don't have to swim," X-Rod said. "You can get there from here."

"How? Isn't Tulum on an island?"

"No. It's a city on the coast. King Xochitl simply went by canoe because it was faster than walking. You can get to Tulum by heading up the beach. I know King Xochitl will want to see you. He was very sad to leave you behind. I overheard him tell one of his men that he wanted to take you but couldn't. He knew that stealing Chilaam's temple dog would start a war."

War! The word jolted me. The monkeys and their coalition were doing everything in their power to start a war between humans. I had to warn Uxmal before it was too late, if someone hadn't already done so. Then I recalled that the people of Tulum made a bone medicine out of orchids. At the very least, I should get some to take back to Fortune-Teller.

"How far is Tulum from here?" I asked.

"If the wind is on your tail feathers, it's a short flight."

"And if you're a little dog walking?"

"Oh," X-Rod said, looking slightly embarrassed. "That's different. If we set out right now, we could be there by sunset."

"We?"

"Your lordship and I. You and me. Us. We two."

"I've made it this far on my own. I can make it the rest of the way."

"I would be honored to escort you to Tulum."

"No thank you." I set out. I didn't want a sea gull escort. I couldn't help thinking about the gull working with the monkeys.

Ignoring me, X-Rod flapped to my side and trotted along beside me, wings folded and mouth open in that peculiar way birds have when they exercise.

"Whadda matter wid youse?" I asked, mocking X-Rod's fake accent. "Don't speak Sea Gull? Dis dog don't wancha."

X-Rod laughed. "Not bad. Your lordship has potential in the dialect department. Mind if I fly? That way I can cover more ground and see what's afoot."

"Take off," I replied, glad to be rid of my unwanted escort.

I followed the shoreline, carefully dodging sharp rocks and odd objects that washed up on shore. I avoided the treeline, knowing monkeys could drop from them and pounce on me with no warning. Little by little, the dense jungle on my left changed to tangled thickets, brushwood, and scrub.

Never having seen the sea, I was thrilled by all the new sights and smells. The water sweeping over the sand tickled my paws. It attacked and retreated, over and over.

Thirsty, I bent my head to take a drink.

"Don't!" X-Rod squawked above me.

Too late. I had already lapped up a mouthful and swallowed. My throat felt like it was on fire, as if I had poured salt down it. I gagged.

X-Rod set down beside me. "I see Your Lordship has never been near the sea before. It's salty and undrinkable."

"What good is all that water if you can't drink it?"

"It's dandy for swimming and it has the most delicious fish!" X-Rod grinned and led me to a pool of spring water in a nearby cove.

I drank deep. Even so, the disgusting taste of brine clung to my throat. I couldn't get rid of it.

I set out again, hoping to reach Tulum before dark.

X-Rod soared into the sky.

Suddenly, an enormous shadow skimmed the ground in front of me.

At first I thought it was my escort, but then I realized it was too big to be X-Rod. Fear gripped me. I looked for a place to hide, but found no cover on the white sandy beach.

The great shadow swooped toward me.

Chapter Thirteen

Toucan landed in front of me. "Hello, Sonny! Sorry I'm late. I heard the whistle and got here as soon as I could. What's the problem?"

"I solved it." *All by myself*, I silently added, proud of myself.

Toucan looked me up and down. "What happened to you? You look positively disgraceful."

"I took Lord Jaguar's suggestion and disguised my fur."

"I must say you did a good job of rolling around in whatever it was you rolled around in." Toucan squinted into the sunbright day and focused on X-Rod floating on air currents. "Good day, Captain!" he yelled.

X-Rod dipped his wings in salute.

"How are Mrs. Gull and the eggs?"

"Due to hatch at any moment," he replied.

I breathed a sigh of relief. So, X-Rod was a good gull and not the one working with the monkeys after all.

Toucan turned back to me. "You and Blue Butterfly gave us some useful information on those cocoa pods. We were able to stop all the bags, with one exception. The city of Tulum received a bag of fake pods yesterday as payment and is understandably upset. It has accused Chilaam of fraud."

"What happens now?"

"We will have to wait and see."

"Something's moving in the jungle," said X-Rod, hovering overhead. "I'm going to check it out." And away he flew.

Toucan and I continued up the beach.

The lush greenery to the left parted. Sword-wielding monkeys wearing coconut shell helmets rushed forward. Beside them, snakes of all sizes and colors whipped through the pure white sand.

Toucan and I made a dash for it, me running up the beach, him taking wing.

Monkeys screeched behind me. One of them grabbed my tail.

I yipped in pain, turned around, and sank my teeth into monkey flesh.

He howled and let go.

Hissing snakes and grinning monkeys surrounded me, blocking my path. They reeked of rotten bananas, coconut milk, and rum.

Inwardly, I quaked in fear, but I managed to put on a brave front.

Toucan set down beside me. "Don't worry, Sonny. X-Rod will bring help."

I hoped he was right. Toucan's expression was hardly comforting. It seemed to say: *We are in big trouble.*

The monkey-and-snake barrier parted, and Copal stepped through. "Well, look what we have here." His evil smile grew. "Two traitors for the price of one."

At his signal, monkeys tied Toucan's wings to his side with vines and wrapped a vine tightly around his long beak.

A monkey clamped a strong hand around my muzzle and gave it a violent shake. "Don't even think about biting me!"

Realizing that resistance was useless, I went limp.

The monkey picked me up and held me against his coarse, uncombed fur.

I hoped I wouldn't pick up any lice.

At Copal's command, we headed south, the way Toucan and I had come. This put the sea on our left. The sun reflecting off the water glittered so brightly it hurt the eyes.

A fast-moving white cloud appeared on the horizon and surged toward us. It darkened the sky and cast an eerie shadow over the sand. After a moment, I realized it was made up of sea gulls—hundreds of them. They carried something in their beaks.

I hoped they were on Lord Jaguar's side. Most birds had joined forces with him, but at least one sea gull was helping Copal.

They dived toward us.

As they got closer, I saw that X-Rod led the charge. I breathed a sigh of relief.

Goldie and some of the other gulls I had just met flew beside him. They raked the monkeys' heads, knocking off the coconut shell helmets.

Copal and his cohorts ducked and swatted at the gulls.

A second wave of birds swooped down, hurling berries and nuts with their beaks.

Monkeys and snakes yipped and ran for cover.

Brightly-colored parrots burst from the greenery to our right and landed behind the monkeys and snakes. They joined wings and beaks to block an escape.

On the left and right, teams of jaguars slinked down the beach, padding toward us with a purposeful gait.

My spirits lifted to see a spotted jaguar approach from one direction and a sleek, black one from the other. Lord and Lady Jaguar were leading the attack.

Snakes curled into defensive positions and hissed, tongues flicking in and out as if licking the air, while monkeys readied their swords.

The jaguars hunkered down, tails twitching, obviously ready to attack. They had no weapons except those nature gave them—sharp claws and equally sharp teeth.

"Drop your swords," Lord Jaguar said in his slow, measured manner of speaking. "Surrender is your only option."

The monkeys glanced around. Blocked by the sea and ringed by birds and jaguars, they seemed to realize there was no way out unless they sprouted wings and flew away. They dropped their weapons. With one hand, they scratched their armpits while using the other to scratch their heads in bewilderment.

My monkey captor set me in the sand. He gave me a condescending pat on the head. "Good doggy."

Although I felt like running to safety, I held my head and tail high and calmly trotted through the monkeys and snakes to Toucan. I gnawed through the vines binding his wings and beak.

"Thanks, Sonny. You're worth your weight in cocoa beans."

"*I'll* say." The voice came from behind me.

I turned.

Lord and Lady Jaguar stood behind me, smiling.

"Nice to see you again, kid," Lord Jaguar said, giving me an affectionate cuff with his paw.

Lady Jaguar licked me with her rough tongue—the cat equivalent of a kiss. "Thank you for saving Agent Blue Butterfly from the spider."

Not knowing what to say, I blushed.

Jaguars passed by carrying sacks of squirming snakes in their mouths. Behind them came Copal in the custody of parrots and dragonflies. Hands bound behind him, mouth gagged, he shot me a look of pure venom.

"What will happen to him?" I asked.

"He'll go back to prison," Lord Jaguar said.

"He's an escaped convict?" I asked, surprised.

"In a manner of speaking," Toucan answered. "Last time, he was sent into exile on Cozumel, an island off the coast near Tulum. Apparently that wasn't far enough away."

"This time," Lord Jaguar said, "we'll send him across the sea to Cuba."

Deep down, I felt sorry for Copal. He had taken a desperate gamble and lost. In doing so, he had adopted all of man's bad habits, including warfare.

But saddest of all—Copal truly believed that man and beast could not live together in mutual harmony and respect.

I knew better.

Chapter Fourteen

I traveled with Lord Jaguar's forces and their prisoners until we reached a finger of land jutting into the sea. Just off the coast lay an island.

"Monkeys hate water," Lady Jaguar said. "This will make the perfect place to keep them until their trial."

Her husband agreed. He turned to Toucan. "We'll set up camp here. Tell the birds to airlift the snakes to the island."

Toucan passed the order to X-Rod who flew off immediately.

"It's time for me to leave," I said. I took the whistle from around my neck and offered it to Toucan.

He shook his head. "Keep it."

"Thank you." I scuffed my paw on the ground. "Well, I guess this is good-bye."

Lady Jaguar smiled sweetly. "You will always be welcome in our den."

"Don't look so sad, kid," Lord Jaguar told me. "It's a big jungle, but we'll run into each other again."

With tears in my eyes, I left and headed north. Not long afterwards, I crossed fields of maize, beans, squash, yucca and sweet potatoes. I hiked past a large number of thatch-roofed huts and small stone houses occupied by farmers, fishermen and hunters dressed in plain white cotton clothing.

I knew I had reached the outskirts of a big city. Was this Tulum? To be certain, I asked an iguana basking on a stone wall.

He lazily rotated his head toward me. "Yeeeeepppppppppp. Tulummmmmmmm is stttrrraaaiiigght ahead."

"Thank you!" I didn't hang around to ask more questions. If I had, I'd have been with the iguana until moonrise.

Three miles later, the heart of the city came into view. Perched high atop limestone cliffs and surrounded by walls about twice a man's height, Tulum looked the way Uxmal described it.

I came to an arched gateway guarded by a soldier. He wore bright, embroidered clothing along with brass wrist and ankle cuffs. He gave me an evil, crooked grin.

Every muscle in my body tensed.

"Come here, Little Dog." He spoke Dog in a voice that dripped honey. His eyes never left me. "You're far from home."

I wondered how he knew that.

"Come on, baby." He rubbed his fingers together as if offering a tasty morsel. "Come to Papa."

My nose told me not to trust this man. Some humans give off an odor of fear; others, affection. The guard reeked of hatred.

I bared my fangs and dared him to come closer.

"If that's the way you want to play it," he said, his voice still cajoling. He lunged at me.

Growling, I dodged out of the way.

A muscular man carrying a stone carver's chisel and hammer walked toward the archway. He paused. "I can sleep well tonight knowing you're keeping the city safe from chihuahuas."

"Shut up and help me catch him," the guard said.

"Forget it. You're on your own, Sea Gull."

Chapter Fifteen

Sea Gull!

In a flash, it all made sense. This was the "sea gull" working with Copal.

I had to find Uxmal and warn him about the traitor! I bolted through the archway. I looked back and blew out a sigh of relief. The soldier was still there. Deserting his post to chase me would have meant death.

In human cities, the upper class—priests, rulers, astronomers, and soldiers—always lived in luxurious palaces near the center of town. That's where I would find Uxmal.

Running as fast as I could, I zipped toward the market so I could get lost in the crowd.

Feet swarmed about me, some wearing leather sandals, some hemp, and some wearing no shoes at all.

I hurried past merchants selling honey, tobacco, vanilla, and rubber.

I left the market and headed uphill. Never had I seen so many altars, temples and shrines. This was clearly a very religious place. I passed a mural in bright orange, blue, and red showing a god standing on his head. A painter was adding yellow highlights.

What a great disappointment Tulum was, in spite of all its temples. It wasn't nearly as grand as Chilaam. Here, everything was built on small, raised platforms. Stone staircases led to simple, flatroofed houses. A tall temple on the east side appeared to be the city's biggest structure.

Where were the magnificent pyramids soaring to the sky? In Chilaam, they loomed so high above the jungle canopy, their tops sometimes disappeared into the morning fog.

Near the edge of a cliff stood the grandest building in Tulum—a limestone temple with a number of levels.

My heart leaped with joy.

At the top of the staircase sat Uxmal, wearing a headdress of quetzal feathers and a tunic of finest cotton.

A jaguar rested its head in his lap and allowed him to spoon something into its mouth.

Beside Uxmal stood a spear-carrying soldier.

I approached cautiously and stopped on the green in front of the temple.

Uxmal looked up and saw me. "Kichi?" He carefully moved the jaguar's head aside and dashed down the staircase. "Kichi!" he exclaimed, squatting in front of me.

I leaped into his open arms.

"My king!" the soldier protested. "He's filthy."

"I don't care!" He cuddled me and whispered in my ear, "You need a bath."

"Uxmal—"

"Xochitl. My real name is Xochitl."

I smiled slyly. "To me, you will always be Uxmal."

He laughed. "If you wish to call me Uxmal, so be it." He looked around and frowned. "Where's Fortune-Teller? Didn't he come with you?"

"No. He's back in Chilaam. Ah Tok and the Emperor of Chilaam plan to attack Tulum."

Uxmal snorted in disgust. "What right have they? If anyone has a complaint, my city does! Chilaam paid us with bags of cocoa pods that were half full of sand!"

"They didn't do it. The monkeys did."

I told him about Shifty the Vulture and his gang of monkeys filling bags with sand to cause a war among the humans.

Uxmal scowled. "The Council of Warriors has advised me to declare war on Chilaam."

"Is Sea Gull on the council?"

"Yes. He's the one pressing hardest for us to attack."

"I overheard Shifty tell the monkeys to take the bags to a sea gull in the palm grove. And a sea gull was going to write a ransom note for me. You have a traitor in your midst, and I think it's that soldier guarding the gate."

A muscle worked in Uxmal's jaw. "That's impossible. Sea Gull is my uncle."

Chapter Sixteen

At that instant, Fou Fou the rhyming Kinkajou, mud-caked and out of breath, ran toward us. "King Xochitl," he gasped out. "An army of humans is approaching."

"Which direction are they coming from?"

"Due south."

"How far away are they?"

"Not far. They will be here by dusk."

Uxmal whirled toward the sun balancing on distant tree tops. "That doesn't give us much time. Sound the alarm," he said to the spear-carrying warrior.

The man, only slightly older than Uxmal, lifted a horn-shaped object to his lips and blew three long ear-piercing blasts.

This, I suddenly realized, was what Uxmal called a conch shell. The night Uxmal was rescued, I had heard a similar sound in the distance.

All activity stopped. The city fell silent.

"An army is approaching!" Uxmal told the crowd that gathered around us. "If your family is beyond the walls, tell them to come here now."

People rushed off to warn of impending danger while merchants in the marketplace stashed their goods in bags. Soldiers ran to their assigned posts.

"It looks like Copal has won after all," Fou Fou said. "There's going to be war between the humans."

"You aren't talking in jingles," I pointed out.

He smiled slyly. "I jingle in the jungle. I only rhyme when I have time."

Uxmal jammed his hands under his armpits, so only his thumbs showed. He scowled.

At first I thought he was watching people pour into the city, but then I followed the direction of his gaze. It burned a path to Sea Gull, still standing by the gateway.

I leaned against Uxmal's leg.

He scooped me up, held me close, and let out a long sigh.

I tried to comfort him by licking his face.

Uxmal patted my head. "Tell me about the monkey that captured you."

I described him in detail.

"My uncle recently owned a monkey like that, but he ran away. What else can you tell me?"

"The monkey's name was Copal and he was fond of coconut milk and rum."

The information made Uxmal's scowl deepen. "That's my uncle's favorite drink. He used to give it to his pet monkey. It looks like I made a big mistake when I taught my uncle how to speak animal languages." He turned to the warrior at his side. "Arrest Sea Gull."

Clearly surprised by the order, it took the man a moment to react. "Yes, my king." He signaled for another soldier to join him. Together, they strode off.

"I wish you were wrong about Sea Gull," Uxmal said, "but you're not. The facts are stacked against him." He ticked them off, starting with his thumb. "One: Sea Gull had a pet monkey named Copal. Two: He just got back from a three-day orchid-gathering trip in the jungle. Three: He speaks Monkey. Four: Sea Gull has the keys to the royal treasury. It would be easy for him to sneak in and exchange sacks of good cocoa pods with bad ones."

"Why would your uncle betray you like this?"

"Sea Gull was next in line to be king until I was born. That put him second in line of succession to the throne. Now that I think about it, he probably had something to do with the attack that killed my mother. I would have perished, had it not been for the jaguar who adopted me. In my absence, Sea Gull became king of Tulum. Years went by. Then, a hunting party from Tulum discovered me in the jungle. My return meant Sea Gull had to step down as king, for I was the rightful heir to my father's throne."

"So Sea Gull did this for power."

Uxmal nodded. "Sea Gull wants to be king of Tulum just as Copal wants to be king of the jungle. You want to know the funny part?" Uxmal asked with a wry smile.

"What?"

"Copal and Sea Gull are working so hard to drive a wedge between humans and animals, but their alliance proves that humans and animals can work together in spite of their differences."

I thought about all the animals I had met along the way. How different we were. A butterfly, a lobster and a dog really didn't have much in common but we had helped each other anyway.

The sun died in the west and a sickly pale moon took its place, shredding wisps of cloud.

When it appeared that everyone was safely inside the city, Uxmal ordered all gateways sealed.

Tension hung in the air, as thick as jungle mist. Fear showed on every face. Uxmal huddled with his advisers. I stayed by his side and admired how desperately he tried to avoid war. Uxmal and I left the advisers and went to a lookout spot on the wall.

Night fell, erasing everything except tiny flickers of light marking distance campfires. It was troubling to see an army ready to attack at first light.

Uxmal snapped his fingers as if a sudden idea had come to him. He called for paper, a pen, a candle, and a piece of string.

A minute later, a warrior returned with them.

By candlelight, Uxmal bent over the paper and wrote.

"What are you doing?" I asked.

"Writing a letter to Ah Tok."

I took a peek at it. "What does it say?" I could understand Human when it was spoken, but I didn't know how to read or write it.

"I asked him to meet me in a neutral location to discuss our differences. Let's see if we can talk him out of this war." He blew a four-note melody on a whistle that looked identical to the one Toucan had given me.

A swallow landed on Uxmal's shoulder.

He warbled that he wished her to deliver a note to Ah Tok. He rolled the paper tight and attached it to her leg with string.

The swallow flew off.

While we waited for her return, I told Uxmal about my trip through the jungle.

He looked at me with a mixture of dismay and admiration. "You followed me all the way here because you thought I had been taken prisoner!"

I nodded. "But my mission changed when I met Lord Jaguar. He told me about a special orchid medicine that's good for the bones. I think it might help Fortune-Teller."

"I'm sure it would. Fortune-Teller is a fine fellow. I'll gladly give him the recipe so he can make his own. On second thought, he could come here as my guest. The medicine works best when you can breathe sea air and bask in the sun."

The swallow returned with a message from Ah Tok. It said, "To King Xochitl: I accept your offer. Meet me on the beach near the palm grove at dawn. Bring the dog."

Chapter Seventeen

At dawn, Uxmal and I stood on the beach under a palm tree. He looked kingly in a bejeweled crown, a finely embroidered tunic, and a cape of quetzal feathers.

Ah Tok strode forward. When he was twenty long paces away he slowed, then stopped. He crossed his arms over his chest. "What kind of trick is this? I agreed to meet with King Xochitl."

"I am he."

Ah Tok flushed in anger. "You? Do you take me for a fool? You're an escaped slave."

"I am no man's slave. When you captured me, I changed my name to Uxmal so you would not know who I was."

Ah Tok rubbed his jaw. "What did you want to talk about?"

"I want to stop this war before it starts."

"You expect me to negotiate with a dog thief? I don't care if you are the king, you stole our sacred temple dog."

"I did not. He followed me home."

"Oh, sure," Ah Tok said, his voice dripping sarcasm. "A little dog travels all this distance through the jungle on his own. That happens every day. I want him back."

"It's up to Kichi to decide whether he stays or goes."

"His name is Sugar."

"He prefers to be called Kichi."

"Oh really? Did he tell you that?"

"As a matter of fact, he did."

"Bah!" Ah Tok said. "Animals don't talk."

"They talk to me," Uxmal said.

"Prove it."

"Tell Ah Tok your name," Uxmal barked.

"Kichi," I replied in Dog.

"When were you born?"

"Two years ago."

Ah Tok snorted in disgust. "So he barks on command. What a cheap trick. I used to have a talking parrot. All he did was repeat what I said."

It looked like the negotiations weren't going very well. I had to convince Ah Tok somehow. What did I know that no one else did? In a flash it came to me. "I know Ah Tok's private name," I barked to Uxmal.

"I can't use that," he barked back, eyes rounding in fear.

A private first name was given at a special naming ceremony when a child was two years old. The name was never made public because it would reduce its power. Only close family members used it. Fortune-Teller used it once in a while.

"You have done nothing to convince me," Ah Tok said, turning to go. "Prepare to be crushed."

"Yaxa," I said. "That's the name." It meant blue.

"Yaxa!" Uxmal blurted.

Ah Tok pivoted. He paled. "What did you say?"

"Your private name is—"

"Don't say it!" Ah Tok said, waving his hand about dramatically. "How did you know?"

"Kichi told me."

"The dog?" Ah Tok's gaze dropped to me.

Uxmal folded his arms across his chest. "Do you believe me now?"

Ah Tok slowly nodded.

"Sometimes things are not as they appear at first glance," Uxmal said. "I did not steal your dog, just as you did not pay with fake cocoa pods. This whole war is a big mistake. We are victims of a scheme to drive man from the jungle." Uxmal explained everything that had happened to him. "We have found the guilty parties and they will be appropriately punished. Let's forget the past. Truce?" Uxmal asked in a hopeful voice.

"I'd say we are even."

Uxmal took off his cape of quetzal feathers and slipped it around Ah Tok's shoulders. "Let this be a symbol that all ill feeling between us is over."

Ah Tok gave him a wry smile. "You were a terrible slave. You make a better king."

They shared a laugh. I felt tremendously relieved to know that the war was over and they were now friends.

Uxmal picked me up and held me so I faced him. "Do you want to go back with Ah Tok?"

I gave him a long lick. "Yes. I miss Fortune-Teller."

Uxmal handed me to Ah Tok. "He misses your brother."

Nodding, Ah Tok tucked me in the pocket of his tunic right over his heart.

"I would like to give you some medicine for Fortune-Teller," Uxmal said. "It will help his bones. Lord Jaguar's mother improved greatly after she moved here. I don't think the jungle with its humidity and dampness is good for the bones. Your brother could come here as my guest and soak up our sunshine."

Ah Tok looked startled by the offer. "I was ready to attack your city. In spite of that, you are willing to help my brother. Why?"

"Not only should man and animal work together and live in peace and harmony, man and man should too."

Chapter Eighteen

Two months later, I sprawled under a palm tree, enjoying the salty breeze and the feel of a cotton blanket beneath me.

The sea, in perpetual motion, washed the beach, leaving interesting shells and creatures on the sand. With Tulum at my back and Fortune-Teller beside me, I had never been happier.

Fortune-Teller was stronger than I had ever seen him. Every day, he drank orchid medicine and rubbed salve on his formerly aching joints.

The priests at Tulum's temples were pleased to have Fortune-Teller as well and had adopted some of the techniques he used to predict the future. Fortune-Teller now served as a diplomat between Chilaam and Tulum and negotiated treaties and trade agreements so that the Almost-War, as it came to be called, would never be repeated. Then, too, he had eyes for the youngest daughter of a temple priest, and she eyed him back.

Yes, things looked good for Fortune-Teller.

Not so for Sea Gull. He had confessed to plotting against Uxmal who showed him mercy and spared his life. In a public ceremony, Sea Gull's hair was cut short to show he was a criminal, and he was exiled to an island far, far across the sea.

Fortune-Teller reached over and stroked my back. "Coming here was a good idea, Kichi."

"I know," I murmured, a small smile curling the edges of my mouth. "How else would you have learned Dog? I tried to teach you, but you were a sorry pupil."

Fortune-Teller laughed. "Maybe Uxmal is a better teacher than you are."

"Very funny. If you're such a good fortune-teller, how come you didn't know that we would end up in Tulum?"

"Maybe I did," he said. "Maybe I knew all along that the Emperor of Chilaam would give you to the King of Tulum as a peace offering."

I opened one eye and studied him a moment, but couldn't tell if he was joking or not.

"You prevented a war," he said, his voice suddenly serious. "There are few dogs and even fewer men who have done what you have."

I was proud of myself for stopping a war. That was a big accomplishment for a little dog!

Historical Note

We know very little about the ancient Mayans. When Spanish conquerors arrived in the 1500s, they destroyed most of their books. Now, only four remain.

There are many unsolved mysteries about the Maya. Recently, archeologists and anthropologists have made a number of exciting discoveries. Previously unknown Mayan cities have been found buried in the jungle undergrowth of Mexico, Guatemala, Belize, and Honduras. Every day, our understanding of the Mayan way of life grows.

From 250 A.D. to 900 A.D., the Mayans created great artwork and amazing buildings. They were ruled by kings and sometimes by queens. In the rain forests of Guatemala, Dr. David Freidel of Southern Methodist University has discovered the 1,200 year-old tomb of a warrior queen.

The ancient Mayan city of Tikal was home to at least 60,000 Mayans. "Downtown" Tikal was about six square miles. Its pyramid soared 212 feet over the jungle floor and was the tallest Mayan structure ever built.

On the east coast of present-day Mexico rests Tulum, one of the most popular tourist sites on the Mayan Riviera.

We once believed that the Mayans were peace loving and did not sacrifice people to their gods. Now we know that this is not true. War was common. Mayan cities often fought each other. They often sacrificed captured enemies to the gods.

One of the mysteries the Mayans left behind is the ball game they played. No one knows the rules or how it was played. We don't even know its name!

Perhaps the greatest mystery of all is what happened to the Mayans. Their historical records end at 909 A.D. when Mayan civilization was at its most glorious. Was there a drought? Famine? War? Disease?

Whatever the cause, Mayan civilization went downhill after 909 A.D.

Like the ancient Egyptians, Mayans used a system of writing called hieroglyphics. They carved important information on stone columns called stellae. Perhaps some day, archeologists will find a stellae that explains the collapse of Mayan civilization.

Chihuahuas are the smallest breed of dog in the world. We think that they are the descendants of the Techichi, a breed of dog that lived in Mexico in the 9th century. Their bones have been found in the graves of noblemen, so we can assume that they were loved and pampered, as they are today.

Pronunciation Guide

A: ah (as in "all")
E: eh (as in "egg")
I: ee (as in "see")
O: o (as in "no")
U: oo (as in "moon")
X: sh (as in "she")
Hu: Wah (as in "Chihuahua")

Ah Tok: ah TOK
Chihuahua: chee-WAH-wah
Tulum: too-LOOM
Uxmal: OOSH-mahl
Xochitl: Sho-CHEE-tul
Yaxa: YAH-shah

For More Reading

Nonfiction Books
Ages 9-12

Baquedano, Elizabeth. *Eyewitness: Aztec, Inca and Maya.* DK Publishing, 2000.

Braman, Arlette, and Michele Nidenoff. *Secrets of Ancient Cultures: The Maya—Activities and Crafts from a Mysterious Land.* Wiley, 2003.

Coulter, Laurie. *Secrets in Stone: All about Maya Hieroglyphs.* Madison Press Book, 2001.

Day, Nancy. *Your Travel Guide to Ancient Mayan Civilization.* Runestone Press, 2000.

Fisher, Leonard Everett. *Gods and Goddesses of the Ancient Maya.* Holiday House, 1999.

Forsyth, Adrian. *Journey through a Tropical Rain Forest*. Simon and Schuster Books for Young Readers, 1989.

Jordan, Shirley. Mayan Civilization: Moments in History (Cover-to-Cover Informational Books: Ancient Civil). Perfection Learning, 2001.

Kallen, Stuart A. *The Mayans (Lost Civilizations)*. Greenhaven Press, 2000.

Keller, Mary Jo. *Aztec Maya Inca Activity Book: Art, Crafts, Cooking, & Historical Aids*. Edupress, Inc., 1999.

Lourie, Peter. *The Mystery of the Maya: Uncovering the Lost City of Palenque*. Boyd Mills Press, 2001.

MacDonald, Fiona. *Step into the Aztec & Mayan Worlds*. Lorenz Books, 1998.

Mann, Elizabeth. *Tikal: The Center of the Maya World*. Mikaya Press, 2002.

Morris, Neil. Everyday Life of the Aztecs, Incas & Mayans (Uncovering History). Smart Apple Media, 2003.

Tutor, Pilar. *Mayan Civilization*. Children's Press, 1993.

Web Resources

http://smu.edu/smunews/waka/default.asp (A wonderful website that tells of the latest discoveries of SMU anthropologist Dr. David Freidel and includes news footage.)

http://www.smm.org/sln/ma/teacher.html#top (The Science Museum of Minnesota maintains this site. It is terrific and loaded with photos.)

http://www.ballgame.org/ (a terrific website about Mesoamerican ball games. Sponsored by the Mint Museums).

http://www.pbs.org/wgbh/nova/maya/ (includes video clips)

Mayan Photo Adventure: http://www.mayaphotoadventures.com/ (John C. Mureiko has given me written permission to use the site. His email address is: john@yohon.cnc.net. His website has wonderful photos of many Mayan sites, including Tulum.)

http://www.mayadiscovery.com/ing/notes/default.htm

http://mayaruins.com/yucmap.html (This site has a useful map. The names of ruins are hotlinks.)

http://www.historylink101.com/1/mayan/ancient_mayan.htm (an excellent source)

Make Your Own Chihuahua

Canon, Inc., provides a design for a paper Chihuahua at: http://cp.c-ij.com/english/3D-papercraft/animal/chihuahua_e.html

About the Author

Lila Guzmán originally translated Nineteenth Century Spanish novels into English, but after a suggestion from her husband, she began writing her own novels as well. Since then, every one of her novels has been an award winner. This is her fifth children's novel and her first with Blooming Tree Press. Visit her at her www.lilaguzman.com.

About the Illustrator

Regan Johnson taught herself to draw horses so she could occupy the time not actually riding them. Now she draws all kinds of things. This is her second book with Blooming Tree Press. Her first book, *Little Bunny Kung Fu*, is currently available.